MONSTER MOVIE

Steve Barlow and Steve Skidmore

Illustrated by Alex Lopez

Franklin Watts
First published in Great Britain in 2016 by The Watts Publishing Group

Credits
Series Editor: Adrian Cole
Design Manager: Peter Scoulding
Cover Designer: Cathryn Gilbert
Illustrations: Alex Lopez

HB ISBN 978 1 4451 4381 1
PB ISBN 978 1 4451 4383 5
Library ebook ISBN 978 1 4451 4382 8

Printed in China.

Franklin Watts
An imprint of
Hachette Children's Group
Part of The Watts Publishing Group
Carmelite House
50 Victoria Embankment
London EC4Y 0DZ

An Hachette UK Company
www.hachette.co.uk

www.franklinwatts.co.uk

Lin

Danny

Sam

"We can't be actors in a monster movie," said Lin. "People will find out we are monsters!"

"We don't have to be actors. I'll work the camera. Sam can work the sound," said Danny.

"OK. But I'll be in charge," said Lin.

Filming started the next day. "Right,"
said Lin. "Britney, you're a little girl,
lost in the woods.

You three are zombies chasing her.

Ready...and action!"

11

"Let's move on," said Lin. "Scene two. It's a full moon. You're turning into a werewolf.

You duck down behind the bench. When you come up — you're a werewolf! Stand by...and...action!"

"OK, the next scene is easy," said Lin. "Jason, you're a demon. You've chased the teenagers to the creepy castle. All you have to do is roar…"

"Like this?" said Jason. "Roar."

Danny shook his head. "No, no.
Like this..."

"Let's give them a real monster movie!" said Lin.

"Yes!" said Danny.

"We'll slay them," said Sam.

A week later the movie was ready.

Sam turned off the lights.

"And now," Lin said, "we proudly present

— our Monster Movie!"

She started the movie...